I Sleep in My Own Bed

WRITTEN AND ILLUSTRATED BY

Glenn Wright

To order additional copies of this book, contact:
Xlibris Corporation
1-888-795-4274
www.Xlibris.com
Orders@Xlibris.com

To Bradley Evan Wright . . .
Daddy loves you,

no matter where

you rest your head.

When it's late at night and dark outside and it's time for me to go to bed,

I change into my pajamas.

And I go to sleep in my own bed.

I go to sleep in my own bed because ...

it's just my size-and made special just for me.

that's where people stay up late and watch TV ... and I can't sleep with the TV on.

I go to sleep in my own bed because…

all my toys are in my bedroom.
I love my toys; they are so cool!

I don't go
to sleep in
my big
sister's
bedroom
because ...

she's weird!

I go to sleep in
my own bedroom
because...

that's where all my clothes are.
They would wonder where I
was if I didn't sleep there.

I don't sleep in my big brother's room because...

And I don't sleep in the bathroom because that would be gross too!

I go to sleep in my own bedroom because . . .

that's where all my stuffed animals are; they are so soft and cuddly. I love them too!

and I think it would make me very dizzy!

I don't sleep in
the refrigerator
because...

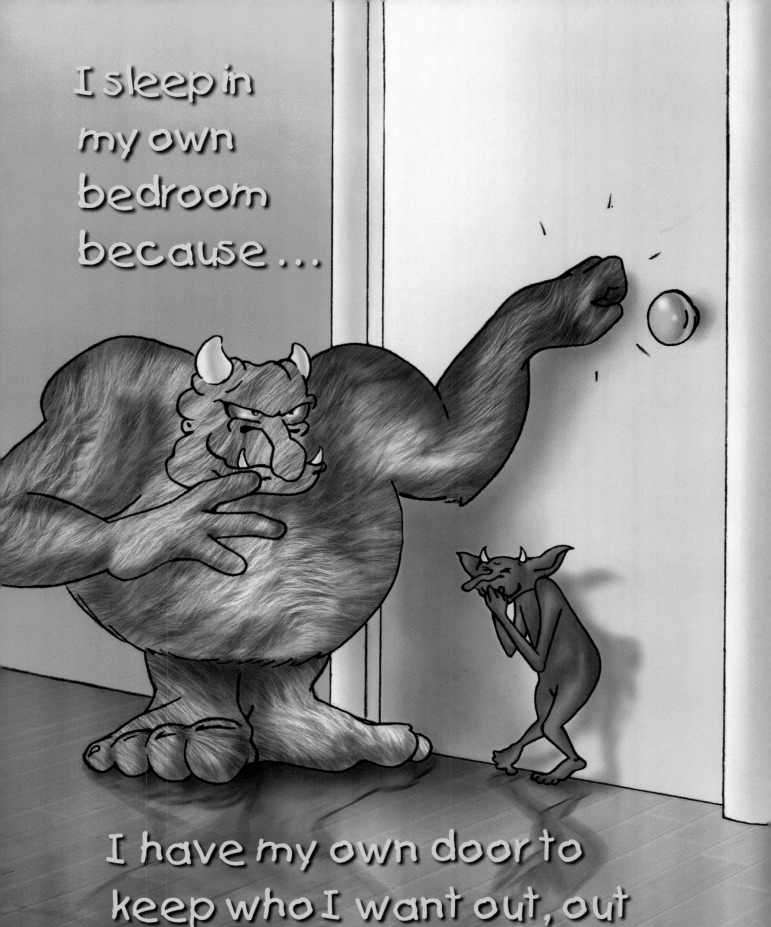

And who I want in, in.

I don't sleep in the
garage because ...

that's where Mommy and Daddy's cars are sleeping!

I don't sleep in
the basement
because...

I sleep in my own bedroom because...

it's painted the colors I like

and has all the cool pictures and
posters of the things I like too!

he's a dog.

Daddy said he was in the doghouse once, but I don't know what he meant!

I go to sleep in my own bed because ...

that's where Mommy and Daddy read to me,

tuck me in,

and give me
a big kiss ...

that's my
favorite part of
sleeping in my own bed!

Good night!

CPSIA information can be obtained
at www.ICGtesting.com
Printed in the USA
LVIW022044250712

291475LV00006B